MY FAVORITE THINGS

RODGERS & HAMMERSTEIN'S

My Favorite Things

ILLUSTRATED BY

RENÉE GRAEF

HarperCollins*Publishers*

For stepparents who guide and nurture their children with love,

especially Maria von Trapp and my own mother Louise

—RG

Raindrops on roses
and whiskers on kittens,

Bright copper kettles
and warm woolen mittens,

Brown paper packages
tied up with strings,

These are a few of my favorite things.

Cream-colored ponies
and crisp apple strudels,

Doorbells and sleighbells
and schnitzel with noodles,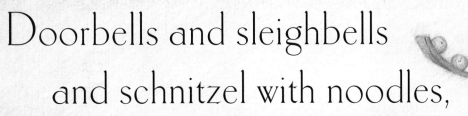

Wild geese that fly with
the moon on their wings,

These are a few of my favorite things.

Girls in white dresses
with blue satin sashes,

Snowflakes that stay
on my nose and eyelashes,

Silver white winters that melt into springs,

These are a few of my favorite things.

When the dog bites,
When the bee stings,
When I'm feeling sad,

I simply remember my favorite things
And then I don't feel so bad.

MY FAVORITE THINGS

Lyrics by OSCAR HAMMERSTEIN II
Music by RICHARD RODGERS

Rain-drops on ros-es and whisk-ers on kit-tens, Bright cop-per

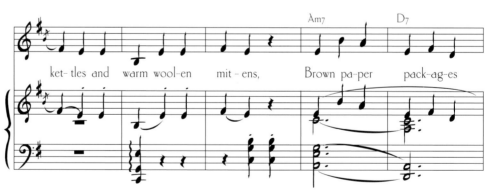

ket-tles and warm wool-en mit-ens, Brown pa-per pack-ag-es

tied up with strings, These are a few of my fa-vor-ite things.

Cream col-ored pon-ies and crisp ap – ple strud-els, Door-bells and sleigh-bells and schnitz-el with noo-dles, Wild geese that fly with the moon on their wings, These are a few of my fa – vor - ite things.

Girls in white dress-es with blue sat-in sash-es, Snow-flakes that stay on my nose and eye-lash-es, Sil-ver white win-ters that melt in-to springs, These are a few of my fa-vor-ite things.

When the dog bites, When the bee stings,

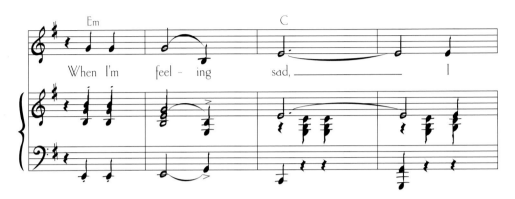

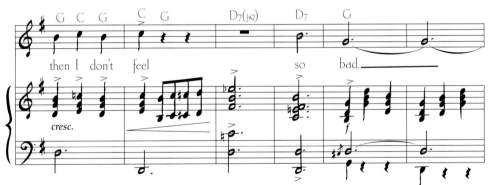
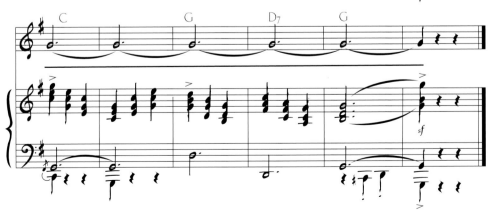